Natalie
the Christmas Stocking Fairy

Special thanks to
Rachel Elliot

ORCHARD BOOKS

First published in Great Britain in 2011 by Orchard Books
This edition published in 2016 by The Watts Publishing Group

3 5 7 9 10 8 6 4

© 2016 Rainbow Magic Limited.
© 2016 HIT Entertainment Limited.
Illustrations © 2011 The Watts Publishing Group Ltd

HiT entertainment

A CIP catalogue record for this book is available from the British Library.

ISBN 978 1 40834 901 4

Printed in Great Britain

MIX
Paper from
responsible sources
FSC® C104740

The paper and board used in this book are made from wood from responsible sources

Orchard Books
An imprint of Hachette Children's Group
Part of The Watts Publishing Group Limited
Carmelite House, 50 Victoria Embankment, London EC4Y 0DZ

An Hachette UK Company
www.hachette.co.uk
www.hachettechildrens.co.uk

Natalie
the Christmas Stocking
Fairy

by Daisy Meadows

ORCHARD

www.rainbowmagic.co.uk

The Fairyland
Palace

Sitting
Room

Holiday Cottage

Fairyland Christmas
Grotto

I'm fed up with Christmas and tinsel galore.
This sweet festive fuss is a drag and a bore.
The fairies have fooled me and made me look bad.
But this year I'll make them feel silly and sad!

This Christmas no stockings will fill up with toys.
No mince pies and candy for good girls and boys.
For I have a plan that will take hope away
And leave stockings empty this dark Christmas Day.

The Magical Mince Pie

Contents

Butter and Bother

"I love making mince pies," said Rachel Walker, sieving flour and salt into a heavy mixing bowl.

"Me too," said her best friend Kirsty Tate, opening the jar of mincemeat and taking a deep sniff. "They have such a Christmassy, spicy smell!"

She put the lid back on the jar and the girls smiled happily at each other. It was the day before Christmas Eve, and they were staying in a cosy holiday cottage in the country with their families.

"Woof!" said Rachel's dog.

"You're looking forward to Christmas too, aren't you, Buttons?" said Kirsty, leaning down to stroke his shaggy head.

"What does the recipe say next?" asked Rachel, as Kirsty washed her hands.

Kirsty turned the page of the recipe book that was propped up on the kitchen counter.

"Rub the butter in with your fingers until the mixture looks like fine crumbs," she read out.

Rachel opened the fridge and then frowned.

"Kirsty, have you already taken the butter out of the fridge?"

"No," said Kirsty in surprise.

"That's funny," said Rachel. "I was sure we had some."

"Maybe we put it somewhere else," Kirsty suggested. "Let's look around."

They hunted high and low, but the butter was nowhere to be found. It was very strange.

"We'll just have to go to the shops again," said Rachel.

"But we're miles from anywhere," Kirsty said with a groan. "And it's nearly closing time."

Just then, Mr Tate walked into the kitchen looking puzzled.

"Hello, girls," he said. "I've just found this pack of butter on Buttons's bed. Don't you need this to make the mince pies?"

"Yes!" exclaimed Kirsty, giving him a delighted hug. "Thanks, Dad!"

"Greedy dog," said Mr Tate with a chuckle, stroking Buttons's head as he left the kitchen.

"That's odd," said Rachel, looking down at Buttons. "He doesn't even like butter."

She rubbed the butter into the flour and then added a little water. Soon she had a ball of golden dough. She wrapped it in cling film and put it in the fridge to chill.

"Shall we add the secret ingredient to the mincemeat now?" Kirsty suggested.

Rachel nodded eagerly.

"It's an old family secret," she said with a smile. "Our own kind of magic!"

The girls giggled happily. They knew more than most people about magic. They were secretly friends with the fairies and had had many adventures in Fairyland.

Kirsty picked up the jar of mincemeat
and tried to unscrew
the lid.

"Oh!" she said in
surprise. "It's stuck!
I must have tightened
it too far when I put
it back on earlier."

Rachel tried to open
the jar, but it was stuck fast.

"Let's ask my dad," she said. "He's
really strong."

They hurried through to the sitting
room. Their parents were playing cards
and listening to carols on the radio.

"Dad, can you undo this?" asked
Rachel, holding out the jar of
mincemeat. "We think Kirsty tightened
it too much earlier."

Mr Walker had to use all his strength to open the jar. At last it popped open and he handed it back to Rachel.

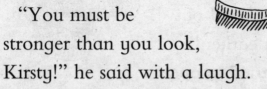

"You must be stronger than you look, Kirsty!" he said with a laugh.

The girls hurried back to the kitchen, keen to add the secret ingredient. But when they reached the doorway, they stopped in amazement.

"What's happened?" Kirsty cried.

All the drawers and cupboards were open and there was flour all over the kitchen. The dough was sitting on the kitchen counter, and it was covered in dirty fingerprints!

Suddenly, Rachel saw the top of a green head poking up from behind the kitchen counter.

"Look!" she exclaimed. "It's a goblin!"

The Christmas Grotto

The goblin gave a squawk of alarm. He flung open the back door and rushed out into the snow.

"Woof!" said Buttons, racing after him.

"Come on!" shouted Kirsty.

The girls followed Buttons out of the back door, just in time to see his tail disappearing around the side of the cottage. When they reached the front garden, they found Buttons standing by the gate, barking loudly.

"Look, Kirsty," said Rachel. "Goblin footprints!"

A trail of long-toed footprints led out of the garden and into the hedge opposite.

"I wonder what a goblin is doing here the day before Christmas Eve," said Kirsty.

"I bet he was up to mischief," said Rachel. "Perhaps Jack Frost sent him. What shall we do?"

"I think we should go to Fairyland right now," said Kirsty in a determined voice. "Jack Frost and his goblins have tried to spoil Christmas before. If they're planning something naughty again, we should tell the Christmas Fairies about it."

Rachel nodded in agreement, and the girls ran back into the cottage. Buttons was barking at their heels. He knew that something was wrong.

"Shh, Buttons," said Rachel. "It's all right. Go and lie down."

As Buttons flopped down on his bed, Rachel and Kirsty hurried upstairs to the little room they were sharing. They closed the door and then opened their lockets. The lockets were presents from the Queen of Fairyland, and were filled with fairy dust.

"This will take us straight to Fairyland," said Kirsty. "Then we have to find the Christmas Fairies as quickly as we can. I'm sure Jack Frost is up to something!"

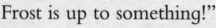

They each took a
pinch of fairy dust
and sprinkled
it above
their heads.
Instantly
the sparkles
whirled around
them, sweeping
them off their feet.
They felt themselves
shrinking inside the cloud of fairy dust.

"We're on our way to Fairyland!"
cried Kirsty in excitement.

Soon the girls found themselves flying
above one of the magical forests of
Fairyland. As they landed among the
snow-topped fir trees, they saw Crystal
the Snow Fairy zooming towards them.

"Hello!" she exclaimed with a beaming smile. "It's wonderful to see you. What's brought you to Fairyland?"

Rachel quickly tried to explain. "We saw a goblin sneaking around our holiday cottage," she said. "We think that Jack Frost might be trying to spoil Christmas again."

"We need to warn the Christmas Fairies!" Kirsty added breathlessly.

"This is serious," said Crystal, looking worried. "I'll take you to them."

She led the way through the forest until they reached a clearing. A little wooden door was set into a grassy bank, and it was standing open as if it were waiting for them.

"This is the Christmas Grotto," said Crystal. "You'll find the Christmas Fairies inside. Good luck!"

"Thank you!" said Rachel and Kirsty together.

Crystal fluttered away, and the girls stepped through the door.

The low grotto ceiling was twinkling with little lights that looked like stars. The smell of berries and spices filled the air. A fire was crackling in the grate and a snug armchair was placed close to the fireplace. Above the grate was a large mirror, which was topped with a sprig of holly. Several stockings were hanging

from the mantelpiece, and a beautiful Christmas tree stood in the corner, dotted with tiny flickering candles. Colourful balloons hung above everything.

"It's beautiful," whispered Kirsty, gazing around.

"Rachel! Kirsty!" exclaimed a tinkling voice behind them. "Oh, thank goodness you're here!"

The Magical Mirror

"It's Cheryl the Christmas Tree Fairy," said Rachel happily.

Cheryl fluttered towards them, holding out her hand. Behind her, they could see Holly the Christmas Fairy, Chrissie the Wish Fairy, Stella the Star Fairy and Paige the Pantomime Fairy.

They were standing around a long table beside a tearful fairy. She had long blonde hair and was wearing a shimmering golden dress with orange netting beneath. Her gold necklace gleamed in the candlelight.

"Is something wrong?" asked Kirsty, hugging Cheryl.

Cheryl looked across at the pretty fairy. The table was covered with torn paper chains and badly wrapped presents. No one looked very happy.

"Let me introduce you," she said,
leading them over to the long table.
"This is Natalie the Christmas
Stocking Fairy."

Natalie smiled at them through her
tears.

"It's wonderful to meet you," she said.
"I've heard so much about you."

Rachel put her arm around the little fairy's shoulders. "What's wrong?" she asked.

"This is where we prepare for Christmas," Natalie said. "Usually it's a really happy time. We sing carols and really enjoy wrapping gifts and making decorations. But this year is different. The decorations keep breaking, the wrapping paper gets torn…we've even lost our box of ribbons. Everything has been going wrong – and now we've found out why."

"Can we do anything to help?" asked Kirsty.

Natalie picked up a little box from the table. It was white, with a gold clasp and a green holly wreath carved on the top.

"This is the box where I keep my three magical items," she said. "Every year, I open it just before Christmas. My magic makes sure all the preparations go well!"

She opened the box, and it started to play *Jingle Bells*. As the music tinkled around the grotto, Kirsty and Rachel peeped into the box.

"It's empty," said Kirsty in surprise.

"Yes," Natalie replied. "When
I opened the box this morning, my
magical items were gone."

She waved her
wand towards
the mirror
above the
mantelpiece.
Tiny silver
snowflakes flew
from her wand
tip and scattered over
the glassy surface of the mirror. When
they faded, the mirror showed Jack Frost
standing in the middle of the grotto. He
was carrying a large sack on his back.

Rachel gave a cry of alarm and turned
around, looking for him. Natalie shook
her head.

"This is a magical mirror," she said.
"It's showing us what happened in here
last night. Jack Frost broke in while we
were all asleep."

The girls watched in horror as Jack
Frost tiptoed around the grotto. When he
saw Natalie's little white box, a horrible
grin spread over his face. He lowered the
sack to the floor.

"Ha!" he whispered, rubbing his bony
hands together. "What have we here?"

He opened the box, and the tinkling sound of *Jingle Bells* filled the air. Jack Frost looked inside, gave a snigger and then tipped the contents of the box into his sack. He threw the box back on to the table.

"This will put a stop to their fun once and for all," he muttered. "Santa's never filled my stocking, so why should anyone else have one?"

He scurried out of the grotto and the picture faded. Kirsty and Rachel exchanged a worried glance.

"We thought he must be up to something," said Kirsty. "We saw a goblin this morning!"

She quickly described seeing the goblin
at the holiday cottage, and the other
fairies looked alarmed.

"Jack Frost could have hidden Natalie's
magical items anywhere," said Paige.
"Where could they be – and how are we
going to find them in time?"

On the Road to the Ice Castle

"We should tell the king and queen," said Stella. "Perhaps they can use their magic to see where Jack Frost has hidden Natalie's items."

"That will take too long," said Natalie. "I have to start searching now – there's not a moment to lose."

"I've got an idea," said Rachel.
"Kirsty and I will stay here with Natalie
and start searching. That way, the rest of
you can go and tell the king and queen
what's happened, and we won't waste
any time."

Natalie turned to her with sparkling
eyes.

"Would you really do that for me?"
she asked.

"Of course," said Kirsty with a smile.
"True friends always help each other
out."

"It's a good
idea," said Chrissie.

"We'll go
to the palace
at once," Holly
added. "Good luck!"

The
Christmas
Fairies
waved
goodbye
and
fluttered out
of the grotto.

"Now we have to decide
where to start looking for the magical
items," said Rachel.

"What *are* the magical items?" Kirsty
asked.

"The enchanted stocking makes sure
that all stockings are ready for Christmas
Eve," said Natalie. "The magical mince
pie makes sure that all mince pies are
tasty and the charmed candy cane
makes sure that stocking gifts are perfect.

But without them, no one will get a Christmas stocking in the human or fairy world."

"That must be why we had such trouble making the mince pies," Kirsty exclaimed.

"If you were Jack Frost, where would you hide the magical items?" asked Rachel.

The girls thought hard.

"I think we should go to the Ice Castle," said Kirsty. "If we can sneak inside, we might be able to find out where Jack Frost has hidden the things he stole, even if they're not actually in the castle."

"Do you really think we should?" asked Natalie. "It could be dangerous. If Jack Frost finds us, he might imprison us."

"We've been there before and escaped," said Kirsty bravely. "Besides, we're not going to let Jack Frost spoil Christmas for everyone!"

"Kirsty's right," said Rachel. "We'll be safe as long as we stick together."

Once out of the grotto, they weaved their way among the trees to the edge of the forest. At last they found themselves on the road to the Ice Castle.

They flew as fast as they could,
keeping their eyes on the glittering castle
in the distance. They were zooming
along so quickly that they almost flew
into two goblins who were arguing in
the middle of the road.

"Look out!" cried
Kirsty just in
time.

They
zipped
sideways
and hid
behind a
clump of
grass at
the edge of
the road, panting.

"That was close!" whispered Rachel.

"Girls," said Natalie in a low voice. "Look at what that goblin has in his hand!"

The girls peeped through the thick fronds of grass and saw the smaller goblin holding up a delicious-looking mince pie and sniffing it.

"That's the magical mince pie!" said Natalie. "I'd recognise it anywhere!"

The goblins were arguing about what was inside the golden pastry.

"It's obviously nettle jam," the small goblin was saying. "That's why it smells so tangy."

"Don't be silly, it's minced seaweed!" the second one snapped. "That's why they're called MINCE pies."

"I can smell the nettles!" shouted the first.

"Well I can smell the sea!" squawked the second.

"Nettles!"

"Seaweed!"

"Nettles!"

"Seaweed!"

Suddenly, Natalie flew out from behind the grass and hovered in front of the goblins.

"Stop!" she exclaimed.

Finders Keepers

"That's my magical mince pie," said Natalie. "Please give it back to me at once!"

The smaller goblin stuck out his tongue.

"Go away, you pesky fairy," he said. "This is mine."

Kirsty and Rachel flew out to join Natalie.

"It's not yours," said Kirsty. "You shouldn't take things that don't belong to you."

"We found it in the Ice Castle," said the smaller goblin.

"Finders keepers, losers weepers," added the other goblin. "We're going to make a whole tray of mince pies for Jack Frost."

Suddenly, Rachel noticed that the end of the smaller goblin's nose was speckled with flour.

"You were in our holiday cottage today, weren't you?" she exclaimed. "What were you doing there?"

The little goblin looked
embarrassed. He scuffed
his long green toes on
the dusty road.

"We just wanted to
know how to make
mince pies," he said.
"But you came back
before I could find out
what was inside."

"That's easy," said
Kirsty. "Mince pies are made
from mincemeat."

"What's that?" demanded the bigger
goblin.

"It's a mixture made of raisins and
currants," said Kirsty.

"And candied orange peel and
lemons," Rachel added.

"And nutmeg and apples," finished Natalie. "Delicious!"

But the goblins were pulling faces. The smaller goblin wrinkled his nose with a disgusted expression.

"Yuck!" he said. "Horrible sweet sickly fairy food."

"What a rotten trick," grumbled the other. "I'm glad we didn't try it!"

Suddenly, Kirsty had an idea. She turned to Natalie and Rachel with shining eyes.

"I think I know how to get the magical mince pie back," she said. "Natalie, could you magic up a special batch of mince pies? They would have to be filled with something the goblins would really like."

"Yes, of course," said Natalie. "But why?"

Kirsty smiled at her and turned to the goblins.

"Goblins, how would you like to have a lovely hot batch of nettle and seaweed pies?" she asked.

Their eyes grew big and the smallest one licked his lips hungrily.

"Natalie could make you as many pies as you can carry," Kirsty went on.

"Yes!" squawked the goblins. "Give us the nettle pies!"

"All you have to do is give us that mince pie you're holding," said Kirsty.

The smallest one thrust the magical mince pie into Natalie's hands. It immediately returned to fairy-size, and Rachel gave a sigh of relief. Then Natalie waved her wand, and a huge tray of steaming-hot pies appeared in front of the goblins. Green ribbons of steam wafted under the girls' noses.

Rachel and Kirsty thought the new mince pies smelled very strange, but the goblins were delighted. They each grabbed several pies and gobbled them down greedily.

"Wonderful!" they cried, spraying crumbs everywhere. "Delicious!"

They rushed off towards the Ice Castle, holding the large tray of pies between them. Natalie turned to the girls with a big smile.

"We did it!" said Rachel, clapping her hands in delight.

"You have helped me so much," Natalie said. "How can I ever thank you?"

"We're happy to help," said Kirsty. "We don't want Jack Frost to spoil Christmas morning!"

"Thank you," said Natalie. "I have to return the magical mince pie to its box now, but will you help me to look for the enchanted stocking and the charmed candy cane?"

"Definitely!" said Rachel, hugging their new friend. "We'll be at the holiday cottage when you need us."

Natalie waved her wand at the girls' lockets. They filled up with fairy dust again, and closed all by themselves.

"I'll see you soon," she said. "And thank you again. I couldn't have done it without you!"

With another wave of Natalie's wand, the girls were showered with silvery fairy dust, which swirled and whirled round them. They held hands as the magic lifted them off their feet to start the journey home. They couldn't wait for their next adventure with Natalie – but right now they had some mince pies to make!

The Enchanted
Stocking

Contents

Snowflakes and Stockings

"What a magical Christmas Eve," said Mrs Walker, sipping her hot chocolate.

Rachel and Kirsty were sharing a large armchair in the conservatory of their holiday cottage. Together with their parents, they had been watching the fluffy white snowflakes tumbling down in the garden. The snow was shining icily in the moonlight, but inside it was warm and snug. Mrs Tate had made hot chocolate with squashy marshmallows for everyone.

"Time for bed, girls," said Mr Tate, smiling at Kirsty and Rachel as they drained their mugs. "Santa will already be on his way."

The girls felt delicious shivers of excitement. Santa was flying through the sky on his sleigh towards them. They felt as if everything was waiting for him – even the snow lying like a blanket over the garden outside.

"I'm sorry that we couldn't find your stockings," said Mr Walker. "It's very odd – I'm sure I unpacked them when we arrived, but now they're nowhere to be seen."

"It doesn't matter," said Rachel, trying not to sound disappointed.

She had never had Christmas without a stocking before. She and Kirsty had hung up their special stockings ever since they were little.

"I expect Buttons has been chewing on them somewhere," said Mrs Tate.

Buttons's ears drooped as he left the
conservatory with the girls. Rachel
stroked his head.
"Don't
be upset,
Buttons,"
she said.
"I'm sure
you had
nothing
to do
with the
stockings
going missing."
"I agree," said

Kirsty, lowering her voice
in case their parents could hear her.
"I think it's happened because Jack Frost
has stolen Natalie's magical items."

Rachel nodded. They had helped
the Christmas Stocking Fairy find her
magical mince pie, but there were still
two items missing, and there were only
a few hours of Christmas Eve left. Time
was running out.

Buttons gave a
curious woof
and darted
upstairs.

"What's
the
matter,
Buttons?"
called
Rachel,
taking a
step after
him.

Kirsty peeped through the open door of the sitting room. It looked very cosy and peaceful. The tree was covered in twinkling coloured lights and the fire was still dancing in the grate, making the whole room glow. It was perfect – except for the bare mantelpiece.

"Somehow it doesn't seem like Christmas Eve without stockings," she said with a sigh.

Rachel had been about to follow Buttons upstairs, but she turned around and came to stand beside her best friend. She slipped her hand into Kirsty's hand and smiled at her.

"We'll make it fun – with or without our stockings," she said in a comforting voice.

Suddenly the girls heard a tiny scratching noise.

"What was that?" exclaimed Rachel.

"It came from the fireplace," said Kirsty, hurrying into the room.

A little fall of soot came down the chimney, and the fire died down.

"Oh no," said Rachel, raising her hand to her mouth. "Do you think that a bird could be stuck in the chimney? I should fetch Dad."

"Wait!" said Kirsty, grabbing her best friend's arm as she turned to leave the room. "I've got a funny feeling that it's not a bird."

The fire died down even more, and
then the girls saw a tiny pinprick of light
shining in the darkness of the chimney.
The light grew brighter
and brighter, and
then a pretty fairy
whooshed down
the chimney in
a whirl of silvery
sparkles.

"Natalie!" said
Rachel happily. "Have
you found your other missing items?"

"Not yet," said Natalie, her cheeks
pink. "But I think I'm very close. I've
followed two goblins all the way from
Fairyland, and I think Jack Frost might
have sent them to hide the enchanted
stocking here!"

Tree
Tricks

"So the enchanted stocking might be very close by?" asked Rachel, feeling very excited. "We've got a really good chance of finding it!"

Natalie fluttered up to stand on the mantelpiece so that she could look into the girls' eyes.

"It might be more difficult than you think," she said.

"Where are the goblins now?" asked Kirsty eagerly.

"That's the trouble," said Natalie. "When I arrived, the snow was so thick and heavy that I couldn't see a thing. I lost sight of the goblins near a tree in the garden. I don't know where they went!"

Her wings drooped a little, and the girls felt very sorry for her.

"Don't give up!" said Rachel. "Show us the tree where you last saw them. Perhaps we can find a clue that will tell us where they went."

Natalie flew down from the mantelpiece and slipped under a lock of Kirsty's hair.

Then the girls tiptoed out into the hall and pulled on their coats and wellies as quietly as they could. They slowly opened the creaky wooden front door and stepped out into the snowy front garden.

"It's lucky that our parents are sitting at the back of the house!" said Rachel with a little chuckle. "They would wonder what we were doing out in the snow so late!"

"Which tree was it?" Kirsty asked Natalie, blinking as the flurries of snowflakes stuck to her eyelashes.

"That one over there," said Natalie, pointing to the apple tree to the left of the house.

The snow was very deep and it was hard to walk through, but at last they reached the apple tree and peered around. There were lots of marks in the snow round the tree.

"Goblin footprints!" said Rachel. "I'd
recognise them anywhere."

"Me too," said Kirsty. "Now all we
have to do is follow the trail of footprints
and we're sure to find the goblins."

"I don't think it's going to be as easy
as that," said Rachel, looking puzzled.
"These footprints don't lead anywhere.
They just go round and
round the tree.
It's as if the
goblins have
completely
disappeared."

She was
right. Kirsty
walked all
the way
round the tree.

She could see the footprints leading up
to the tree, and going round it. But there
were no footprints leading away.

"It's impossible!" she said. "Goblins
can't fly."

She looked round, wondering if the
goblins were watching them from the
dark bushes that bordered the garden.

"Did you see anything else that might
give us a clue about
the goblins?"
Rachel asked
Natalie.

The little fairy
thought hard.

"The only other
thing I noticed were
some scratching noises as
I came down the chimney," she said.

"But they were coming from upstairs inside the cottage. How could the goblins have got inside the house without leaving footprints here?"

"I know!" said Kirsty, turning to them with shining eyes.

She had been staring thoughtfully at the tree, and suddenly she had realised what must have happened.

"The goblins didn't leave any footprints because they never left the tree," she said.

"I don't understand," said Rachel. "If they never left, then why can't we see them?"

"Because they climbed *up* the tree instead!" Kirsty exclaimed.

She pointed upwards to where a branch of the tree rested on a window ledge. The window was open.

"You're right – that's how they got into the cottage!" Natalie said. "Which room is that?"

Rachel and Kirsty exchanged worried looks.

"It's our bedroom!" cried Rachel. "Come on!"

Tug of War

The girls started to run back to the house, but it was slow-going in the deep snow. It seemed to take ages before they reached the front door. They flung off their snowy coats and wellies, and raced upstairs to their bedroom.

The bedroom door was open, and they could hear Buttons growling from inside.

They rushed in, and then stopped in
astonishment.

Two goblins were sitting on the
windowsill, clutching the girls' Christmas
stockings and
squawking in
fury. Buttons
was hanging
on to the
other ends of
the stockings,
growling
deep in his
throat. The
goblins were
wrapped up in
woolly scarves, and
one of them clearly had a cold, because
his nose was very red. Their bony feet

were reaching out for the topmost
branches of the apple tree.

"They're trying to get away!"
exclaimed Rachel. "Good boy, Buttons!"
The girls raced across the room to
help Buttons, but Natalie gave a cry of
surprise and flew towards
the goblins.

"That's not
a hat!" she
exclaimed,
pointing
at the
goblin
with the
red nose.
"That's the
enchanted
stocking!"

"That doesn't belong to you!" cried
Rachel. "Give it back!"

"Leave us alone, horrible human
girls!" screeched the red-nosed goblin.
"A-CHOO!"

Rachel and Kirsty grabbed the ends of
the stockings and pulled as hard as they
could. There was a loud ripping sound.

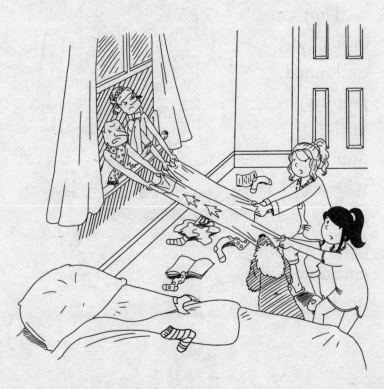

"Oooh. Three against two!" squealed the other goblin. "Not fair!"

"Pull!" yelled Kirsty.

"Heave!" bawled the goblins.

The strange tug of war continued, but the goblins were struggling to stay on the windowsill. The girls and Buttons gave one pull and the goblins came tumbling inside the room, still clinging to the stockings. Rachel, Kirsty and Buttons all fell backwards, panting, and the goblins landed on top of them.

89

"Ouch!" said Kirsty, pushing the red-nosed goblin off her leg.

"Get your elbow out of my eye!" moaned the other goblin to Rachel. Everyone sat up and tried to catch their breath. The goblins pulled off their scarves. Natalie perched on Rachel's knee. "Why are you being so naughty?" she asked the goblins. "You've stolen my enchanted stocking, and now you're trying to steal Rachel and Kirsty's stockings too."

"That was a really mean thing to do," said Kirsty. "You shouldn't take things that don't belong to you."

"And you shouldn't spoil things that other people care about," Rachel added, holding up the ripped stockings and gazing sadly at them. "These were our favourite stockings and you've ruined them. They'll take ages to mend."

"Ruined?" exclaimed the red-nosed goblin, sniffing scornfully. "They're perfect! They're the best stockings I've ever seen. Not like this silly thing."

He pointed to the enchanted stocking, which was still on his head. Rachel and Kirsty felt puzzled. "You mean, you *want* stockings that are ripped and spoiled?" asked Rachel in confusion. The other goblin rolled his eyes at her. "Of course we do, stupid!" he said rudely. "Neat, clean stockings are for girls and fairies. Brave, handsome goblins like me want stockings like these."

"So that's what you were doing here?"

asked Natalie. "You were looking for stockings to hang up for Santa?"

"None of your business," said the red-nosed goblin, sticking out his tongue at her and giving another loud sneeze. "Anyway, why shouldn't we have stockings? Jack Frost's got one, so we should have them too."

The goblins started to move towards the window, wrapping their scarves around their necks.

"I've got an idea," whispered Kirsty to Rachel. "I think we can get Natalie's enchanted stocking back, but it means that we have to give away our own Christmas stockings!"

Stocking Swap

"If it helps Natalie, then I'll happily give away my stocking," Rachel replied at once. "After all, Christmas isn't just about the presents that Santa brings."

Kirsty smiled at her.

"I thought you'd say that," she said. "If we can persuade the goblins to give us the enchanted stocking in return for our stockings, we might still be able to stop Jack Frost spoiling Christmas."

The girls looked at the goblins. They were just about to climb out of the window, and were shoving each other, bickering and sounding very grumpy.

"Wait!" Kirsty called. "Please come back."

The goblins looked around in surprise.

Rachel and Kirsty held out their stockings.

"Would you like to do a swap?" asked Rachel.

"What do you mean?" asked the red-nosed goblin in a suspicious voice.

Kirsty took a deep breath. "If you'll give Natalie her enchanted stocking, we'll give you our ripped stockings," she said.

Natalie looked at the girls in astonishment. She hadn't heard their plan, but she knew how much their stockings meant to them. She could hardly believe her ears!

The goblins took a step towards the girls.

"Really?" asked the red-nosed one, taking the enchanted stocking off his head and holding it in his hands. "You'd really swap this horrible thing for those lovely stockings?"

"Don't believe them!" squawked the other goblin,

tugging on his arm. "It's a trick! They're fibbing!"

"It's not a trick, and we always tell the truth," said Rachel. "Give us the enchanted stocking and I promise that you can have these stockings to keep."

The goblins
went into the
corner and
whispered to
each other
for a long
time. The girls
couldn't hear
anything except an
occasional sneeze. Natalie fluttered onto
Rachel's shoulder and they waited.

At last the goblins turned around, and
Rachel and Kirsty held their breath.

"We agree!" said the goblins together.

Smiling, Natalie flew over to them and
they handed her the enchanted stocking.
It returned to fairy-size as soon as she
touched it. Then Rachel and Kirsty gave
their ruined stockings to the goblins.

"Hee hee!" squealed the red-nosed goblin in delight. "We've got two stockings for one! Those silly humans don't know how to bargain. A-CHOO!" He capered around the room, waving his ripped stocking above his head.

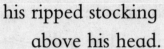

"Come on," said the other goblin in an impatient voice. "Let's go." They sprang out of the window onto the branches of the apple tree and disappeared into the darkness. Rachel and Kirsty looked at each other in delight.

"We did it!" said Kirsty. "Now there's only one magical item left to find."

But Natalie didn't look as happy as they expected.

"It's wonderful that we've found the enchanted stocking," she said. "But it's almost Christmas Day, and the charmed candy cane is still missing. Without it, the boys and girls won't get any sweets this Christmas."

"We'll think of something," said
Rachel kindly. "But first, let's make
sure that those goblins are really leaving.
I don't want them to get up to any more
mischief here!"

They hurried over to the window
and leaned out as far as they dared.

Outside in the garden, they could see the
two goblins clambering down the tree
trunk. Their green skin gleamed in the
moonlight.

"You're going too slowly," one of them complained. "Hurry up."

"Get your foot out of my eye," grumbled the other one. "I'm going as fast as I can. What's the big rush, anyway?"

"I want to try some of that stripy candy that Jack Frost brought back," said the first goblin. "If we're not back soon, the other goblins will have eaten it up."

"You're right," said the other, speeding up. "They're all really greedy. A-CHOO!"

Natalie and the girls gazed at each other in excitement.

"Do you think they're talking about the charmed candy cane?" asked Natalie.

"Yes!" said Kirsty. "Jack Frost must be keeping it close beside him – right in the heart of his Ice Castle!"

A Sweet Surprise

The girls closed the window and Natalie hovered beside them. Jack Frost's castle was a scary place, and there was very little time left. Could they get the charmed candy cane back before the sun rose?

"We should leave now," said Rachel, thinking aloud. "Every moment is precious."

"No," said Natalie. "You shouldn't have to help me get into Jack Frost's castle on Christmas Eve. I'll go by myself."

"No way," said Kirsty in a determined voice. "We're not letting you go there alone."

"Kirsty's right," said Rachel. "We're coming with you."

Natalie could see that she wouldn't be able to change their minds. She smiled gratefully.

"Thank you," she said. "It will be nicer to have you there with me. I'll make sure that time stands still here while you're gone, so your parents won't realise that you're not in bed."

Rachel knelt down beside Buttons and patted his shaggy head.

"You were wonderful, Buttons!" she said. "Thanks to you, the enchanted stocking is safe."

"I'd like to thank him too," said
Natalie.

She waved her wand and cast a
magic spell.

"A loyal pet whose heart is true.
Girls whose hearts are generous too.
Give my dog and human friends
Presents that will make amends."

There was
a puff of
sparkling fairy
dust. When
the sparkles
cleared, a juicy
bone was lying
between Buttons's
front paws.

But he wasn't the only one to be surprised with a gift. Kirsty and Rachel found that two beautiful new stockings had appeared in their hands. They were delicately embroidered with pictures of the girls' fairy friends.

"Thank you!" said Rachel in wonder.

"I've never seen such beautiful stockings!" Kirsty added.

"When Santa sees them, he will know that you are friends with the fairies," said Natalie.

"Let's go and hang them up before we go to the Ice Castle," said Rachel eagerly. "Come on, Buttons!"

Rachel and Kirsty tiptoed downstairs. Buttons ran ahead of them and flopped down in his bed with his bone. The girls could hear their parents talking in the conservatory. They crept into the sitting room and carefully hung their wonderful new stockings from the mantelpiece.

"There's just one more thing to do before we go," said Kirsty, looking at Rachel.

"Oh yes!" said Rachel, remembering. "Santa and his reindeer will be hungry when they arrive."

They hurried into the kitchen and opened the tin of mince pies that they had made the day before.
Rachel put three
mince pies
on a plate
while
Kirsty
took some
carrots
from
the
fridge.

Then they put the treats on the
mantelpiece beside their stockings.

"Ready?" asked Natalie.

Kirsty and Rachel held hands.

"Ready!" they said together.

With a swish of Natalie's wand,
the girls began to shrink into fairies,
surrounded by shimmering snowflakes.

Gauzy wings appeared on their backs, and they felt Natalie's magic whisking them away to Fairyland. The final part of their adventure was about to begin!

The Charmed
Candy Cane

Contents

Back to Fairyland

Rachel, Kirsty and Natalie arrived
outside the Christmas Grotto in a
flurry of sparkles. The three friends
hurried inside and Natalie returned the
enchanted stocking to her little white
box. Then she magicked up snug coats
and boots for Kirsty and Rachel.

"Are the other Christmas Fairies here?" asked Rachel, hoping to see some of their friends again.

"No," said Natalie. "They're all at the palace with the king and queen. The night before Christmas is a very busy time for us. They're relying on me to find the last missing object."

"Not just you," said Kirsty, smiling at the little fairy. "Rachel and I are here to help you."

"Besides, there's no time to fly to the palace and ask for help," Rachel added. "It's almost midnight."

"If we can't get the charmed candy cane back before Christmas Day, no one will get any sweets in their stockings this year," said Kirsty. "We have to get to the Ice Castle and find out where Jack Frost has hidden it. There's no time to lose."

They hurried out of the Christmas Grotto and fluttered up into the cold night air. After they had made their way through the trees, they reached the moonlit road to the Ice Castle.

"We have to fly like the wind," said
Natalie.

With her wand she tapped first
Rachel's wings, then Kirsty's and
finally her own.

"Now you will be able to fly three
times as fast as before!" she said.

The girls fluttered their wings and shot
forward at an incredible speed.

"It's like the best fairground ride ever!"
squealed Kirsty as they zoomed forward.

Within a few minutes they were hovering high above the castle. There were goblins on patrol all around the battlements.

"We'll never get in while the guards are watching," said Natalie.

"Let's fly lower," said Rachel. "We might spot an unguarded way in if we get closer."

The three fairies peered around in the moonlight.

"I can't see any way in," said Natalie.

Her breath was like mist in the freezing night air.

"Kirsty, do you remember when we came here with Holly?" said Rachel. "We found an open trapdoor. Perhaps we could get in that way again."

Kirsty looked around eagerly, but then her shoulders slumped.

"I can see the trapdoor," she said, pointing at the icy floor of the battlements. "But there are two goblin guards standing right on top of it."

It looked as if it was going to be impossible to get in. But as Rachel was staring at the goblins on top of the trapdoor, she noticed something strange.

"Do those goblins look a bit odd to you?" she asked.

They flew a little lower. The goblins looked bigger than usual, and barely a scrap of green skin could be seen.

"They're completely wrapped up against the cold!" realised Rachel. "Look – the one on the left has feathers wrapped over the top of his head."

"The other one's wearing three fake beards," added Kirsty with a giggle.

All the goblin guards on the battlements were the same. It was so cold that they had put on anything they could find. The girls could see blankets, turbans, sombreros and deerstalkers. There was even one in an old-fashioned diving helmet. Each of the goblins was wrapped in a big scarf.

"I'm still freezing," they heard one of the goblins grumble.

He was wearing a top hat that was so big that it was resting on his shoulders.

His voice was very muffled.

"It's lucky we found that old dressing-up box," said another from beneath a three-cornered pirate's hat.

"Jack Frost's really mean to make us work when it's so cold," said another. "I can't see a thing."

Rachel and Kirsty looked at each other in excitement.

"That's how we can get in!" said Kirsty. "They're so wrapped up that they might not spot us flying in."

"Let's try it," said Rachel eagerly. "We just have to be very, very quiet."

A Chilly Search

Soundlessly, the three friends fluttered down towards the courtyard. Rachel and Kirsty kept their fingers crossed as they drifted lower, hoping that the guards wouldn't notice them. At last they felt the hard stone beneath their feet. They had done it!

"Where shall we start looking?" asked Natalie in a whisper.

Her voice shook a little. Rachel and Kirsty had visited Jack Frost's Ice Castle several times, but she had never been there before. It was a dank and dismal place. Rachel gave her hand a comforting squeeze.

Kirsty looked around and saw a corridor leading off from the courtyard.

"Let's start down there," she said in a soft voice.

They fluttered down the corridor. It was lit by flickering torches, and there were many doors on each side of it. At the far end was a winding staircase.

"We'll have to search every room," said Natalie. "Jack Frost could be keeping the charmed candy cane anywhere."

"Let's split up," Rachel suggested. "We'll search more quickly if we separate."

The fairies checked all the rooms along the corridor. They found plenty of cobwebs and lots of balls of dust, but no charmed candy cane.

They met up at the end of the corridor.

"Any luck?" asked Natalie.

Rachel and Kirsty shook their heads.

"Let's go up this staircase," Kirsty suggested. "Perhaps he's hidden it in one of the towers."

They fluttered up the narrow, spiralling stairs.

At the top they found another corridor
and another staircase.

"Let's keep searching," said Natalie.
"But keep a sharp lookout for goblins!"

The girls split up again and started to
search. They fluttered up staircase after
staircase, through corridor after corridor
and into room after room. They saw the
open dressing-up box that the goblins had
raided. They saw the drums and guitars
that belonged to the Gobolicious Band.
They saw the tutus and headdresses that
the Goblinovski Festival Ballet dancers
wore. But they didn't see a single sign of
the charmed candy cane. As they arrived
at the end of another corridor, Kirsty
drew in her breath sharply.

"I can hear goblin voices!" she said
urgently. "Quick – hide!"

It was so cold inside the stone walls of the castle that icicles were hanging from the ceilings. Rachel, Kirsty and Natalie hovered behind three of the thickest icicles as the goblins hurried along the corridor below.

"Jack Frost's eaten all the bogmallows *again*," grumbled the smaller goblin, who was wearing a chef's hat. "He's ordered me to make another batch.

I'm bored of always making bogmallows
and never eating them."

"I just wish he'd let us wear warmer
clothes indoors," said the other. "My toes
are turning into icicles!"

They disappeared down the stairs and
the girls heaved sighs of relief.

"Phew, that was close," said Rachel.
"Come on."

They flew up the
stairs and found a
single wooden
door at the
top. They
had reached
the topmost
room of
the highest
tower.

"It has to be in here," said Natalie. There were all sorts of things piled up around the room. Rachel, Natalie and Kirsty searched through mouldy plates, uncared-for ornaments, chipped mugs and smelly socks. Eventually, they stopped and looked at each other in disappointment.

"Nothing," said Kirsty. "That means there's only one room in the castle that we haven't checked."

"I was afraid you were going to say that," said Rachel.

"What do you mean?" asked Natalie. "Where do you think it is?"

"It must be in the Great Hall," Kirsty told her.

"That's great!" said Natalie. "Let's go and find it."

"If only it were that easy," said Rachel with a sigh. "You see, the Great Hall is where Jack Frost will be!"

Bogmallows and Bad Tempers

Kirsty and Rachel led the way to the Great Hall. As they flew closer, they heard many running footsteps and the squawking sound of goblin voices. The door of the Great Hall banged loudly as goblins hurried in and out. Every time the door opened, the three friends could hear Jack Frost bellowing orders at the top of his voice.

"Where are my bogmallows?"

"Get me an extra blanket!"

"Shut that door!"

The three fairies hovered close to the ceiling.

"How are we going to get inside?" asked Rachel.

Before her friends could reply, they saw a worried-looking goblin running down the corridor towards the Great Hall. He was carrying a tray of bogmallows, and the girls realised that he was the goblin they had seen earlier. He was still wearing his chef's hat.

The goblin's hands were full, so he used his elbow to turn the handle and open the door. He pushed it as hard as he could and it swung open.

"Quickly, let's follow him in!" said Kirsty.

The door opened and the goblin hurried through with his tray. As the door began to close behind him, Kirsty, Rachel and Natalie darted inside.

Jack Frost was sitting on his throne, surrounded by a semi-circle of goblins. In the corner, a withered branch had been stuck into a Christmas tree pot, and a few scrappy paper chains were looped around it. Three goblins were standing around the tree, holding carol sheets. Their loud squawks were obviously their idea of singing, but it was a terrible noise. Kirsty put her hands over her ears.

"I think they're all singing different carols," she groaned.

"Let's stay out of sight," said Rachel. They fluttered up to the ceiling and perched on the chandelier so that they had a good view of the hall. At that moment the goblin carrying the tray stepped up to the throne and bowed low.

"Your bogmallows, Sire," he said.

"You took your time!" snapped Jack Frost rudely. "Give them to me."

He snatched the tray and started to gobble the bogmallows.

The goblins around him shuffled closer to the throne. They looked hungry, but their leader ignored them.

As Jack Frost was stuffing the bogmallows into his mouth, another gaggle of goblins was trying to light a fire in the grate. They didn't seem to know what to do, and Rachel and Kirsty watched them with interest.

"You have to rub things together," one of them was saying bossily. "I heard a Boy Scout say so."

The others started to make suggestions.

"Hands?" said one.

"Bogmallows?" said another.

"Balaclavas?"

"Noses?"

"Wellies?"

A plump goblin started busily rubbing two old toothbrushes together.

"It's not working," he moaned.

Suddenly Natalie noticed something.
The goblins who were sitting around
the throne were all drooling. She looked
more closely, and saw that their eyes
were fixed on one of the arms of Jack
Frost's throne.

"That's strange," she murmured.

At that moment Jack Frost moved, and the folds of his cloak fell aside. Tucked down the side of the throne was a long, scrumptious-looking striped sweet with a curved handle. Natalie clutched Kirsty's arm and pointed.

"It's the charmed candy cane," she whispered. "We've found it!"

A Charmed Rescue

"Look!" whispered Kirsty. "One of the goblins is trying to take the charmed candy cane."

The goblin reached out towards the sweet treat, but Jack Frost saw him and rapped the greedy hand with his wand.

"OOOH!" yowled the goblin.

"Leave it alone!" bawled Jack Frost. "You're not scoffing that – it's mine!"

He went back to munching on the bogmallows. His face got closer and closer to the tray as he scooped them into his mouth.

"Another goblin's trying to take it now," said Rachel.

But this time, Jack Frost didn't notice.

Carefully, the goblin lifted it from the arm of the throne. He carried it slowly towards his open, drooling mouth. "Oh no, he's going to eat it!" Natalie groaned.

The goblin holding the charmed candy cane stuck out his tongue and took a long, slurpy lick.

"Yuck!" squawked the goblin. "Disgusting!"

He thrust the charmed candy cane away from him, and

another goblin grabbed it and took a lick.

"UGH!" he squealed. "Strawberries and cream!"

"We have to stop them licking it," said Natalie in a frantic voice. "There are so many goblins that if they all liked it, the candy cane would be completely eaten!"

"Perhaps we could take them by
surprise and snatch it away from them,"
suggested Kirsty. "If we all pull together,
we might be strong enough."

"It's worth a try!" said Rachel.
"Let's go!"

They swooped down from the
chandelier as the charmed candy cane
was passed from goblin to goblin. Each
of them took one lick and then pulled a
revolted face.

"I wanted it to taste
like rotten tomatoes,"
wailed one.

"I was hoping
it'd taste like
mouldy custard,"
said another
disappointedly.

As he thrust the charmed candy cane at the next goblin, Rachel, Kirsty and Natalie threw their arms around its curved handle.

"Pull!" cried Rachel.

The three friends pulled with all their might, and the surprised goblin squawked in alarm, hanging on to the end.

"Let go!" he squealed. "Help! Fairies!"

Jack Frost turned, gave a furious yell and grabbed the stripy sweet, shaking it as hard as he could. The three fairies were sent spinning away into the corner of the Great Hall.

"This is mine!" Jack Frost bellowed, taking a big lick of the handle. "And I'M going to eat it!"

"No!" cried Natalie.

"Ha ha!" Jack Frost laughed. "You can't stop me!"

He took a great big
lick…

"ICK! ACK!
UGH!" he spat.
"It's foul!"

He flung it away
and it skidded
into the corner
where the fairies had
landed. It came to a
stop beside them, and Natalie
returned it to fairy-size at once.

"Yes!" exclaimed Rachel and Kirsty
together.

Natalie raised her wand to return them
to the Christmas Grotto, but then she
paused and looked at Jack Frost. He had
slumped down into his throne, looking
very miserable.

"You might as well go," he told them. "I should have known that my plan wouldn't work."

"What do you mean?" asked Rachel.

"Nothing ever goes right for me," Jack Frost mumbled. "I've never had a stocking at Christmas, and this year's going to be just the same."

He pulled a large spotted handkerchief out of his pocket and blew into it noisily. The goblins stared at him in astonishment.

"He looks really miserable," said Kirsty.

"I almost feel sorry for him," added Natalie.

"Me too," said Rachel. "But what are we going to do about it?"

The three friends looked at each other.

"We can't leave him unhappy at Christmas," said Kirsty firmly.

"But we can't let him have the charmed candy cane either," Rachel replied.

"It's OK," said Natalie with a little smile. "I've got an idea."

Stockings and Sleigh Bells

Natalie raised her wand and chanted a magic spell.

"*Mince pies, stockings, candy cane,*
Back where they belong again.
Girls and boys from east to west
Get the sweets they like the best.

Santa, hear my Christmas plea,
Fill each stocking that you see.
Let this castle, cold and grey,
Be full of joy on Christmas Day."

Tiny sparkling snowflakes whooshed out of her wand like a fountain. The  sparkles whirled around the Great Hall, touching each goblin and finishing in the hands of Jack Frost. When the sparkles cleared, every goblin was holding a horrible, holey stocking. On Jack Frost's lap was a large blue stocking decorated with bolts of lightning.

The goblins jumped around in excitement, and a big smile spread over Jack Frost's face.

"I hope that they all have fun opening their presents together," said Natalie. "At Christmas, one of the most important things is to have a good time with your family and friends."

"I agree," said Kirsty. "And now we've found the charmed candy cane, I think it's time for us to go back to our families."

"And it's time for me to take the charmed candy cane back to the Christmas Grotto," said Natalie. "Thank you so much for helping me to find my magical items."

She put her arms around them and they hugged tightly.

"We're just glad that we found them in time," Rachel replied. "Merry Christmas, Natalie!"

"Merry Christmas, both of you," said Natalie, her eyes shining. "I don't need to cast a spell to know that you are going to have a wonderful Christmas Day."

She waved her wand and a whirl of fairy dust surrounded Rachel and Kirsty, lifting them off their feet.

"Goodbye, Natalie!" called Rachel. "Goodbye, Jack Frost!"

When the sparkles cleared, Rachel
and Kirsty's warm coats were gone, and
they were back in the peaceful sitting
room of the holiday cottage. The lights
were twinkling and they could hear their
parents chatting in the conservatory.

Rachel looked at the clock. "It's almost
midnight, just like when we left," she
said. "No time has passed since we went
to Fairyland."

The sitting room door creaked and
opened slowly. Buttons
ran in, wagging his
tail. He licked
their hands,
delighted to see
them.

"Do
you think
he knows
that we've
been on an
adventure?'
asked Kirsty.

"Of course he knows, " said Rachel,
kneeling down and patting him. "He's
a very clever dog."

Suddenly, Kirsty gave a little cry
of excitement.

"Rachel, look at the mantelpiece," she whispered.

In the orange glow from the fire, they could see that the plate of mince pies had been replaced by a few crumbs. The stockings hanging above the fire were bulging, and there was a feeling of magic in the air. Santa had been!

Both girls reached out to their
stockings, and then they paused.
They looked at each other.

"Shall we wait until the morning to
open them?" asked Rachel.

"That's just what I was thinking,"
Kirsty said. "It'll be much more
Christmassy to open the presents with
our mums and dads."

They smiled at each other and then tiptoed out of the sitting room, with Buttons following them. As they were walking up the stairs to their bedroom, Kirsty stopped and touched Rachel's arm.

"Listen," she whispered.

In the distance they could hear the faint tinkling of sleigh bells. Santa was on his way to visit someone else. Rachel gave a happy sigh.

"This has been one of the most Christmassy Christmas adventures we have ever had," she said. "Merry Christmas, Kirsty!"

Now Kirsty and Rachel
must help...

Keira the Film Star Fairy

Read on for a sneak peek...

"Look, there's Julianna Stewart!"
whispered Kirsty Tate. "Isn't her fairy
princess costume beautiful?"

Rachel Walker peeked round just as
Julianna walked past. The film star gave
the girls a friendly wink, then sat down
in a director's chair with her name on
the back to study her script.

"Who'd have thought a world-famous
actress like Julianna would come to
Wetherbury village?" said Rachel.

"And who'd have thought that she'd be
spending most of the school holidays in

Mrs Croft's garden?" added Kirsty.

Mrs Croft was a friend of Kirsty's parents, a sweet old lady who had lived in Wetherbury for years. Her little thatched cottage with pretty, blossoming trees at the front often caught the eyes of tourists and passers-by. A few weeks ago when Mrs Croft had been working in her garden, an executive from a big film studio had pulled up outside. He wanted to book the cottage for a brand new film starring the famous actress Julianna Stewart. When Mrs Croft agreed, she became the talk of the village...!

Read Keira the Film Star Fairy to find out what adventures are in store for Kirsty and Rachel!

Calling all parents, carers and teachers!
The Rainbow Magic fairies are here to help
your child enter the magical world of reading.
Whatever reading stage they are at, there's
a Rainbow Magic book for everyone!
Here is Lydia the Reading Fairy's guide to
supporting your child's journey at all levels.

Starting Out

1

Our Rainbow Magic Beginner Readers are perfect for first-time readers who are just beginning to develop reading skills and confidence. Approved by teachers, they contain a full range of educational levelling, as well as lively full-colour illustrations.

Developing Readers

2

Rainbow Magic Early Readers contain longer stories and wider vocabulary for building stamina and growing confidence. These are adaptations of our most popular Rainbow Magic stories, specially developed for younger readers in conjunction with an Early Years reading consultant, with full-colour illustrations.

Going Solo

3

The Rainbow Magic chapter books – a mixture of series and one-off specials – contain accessible writing to encourage your child to venture into reading independently. These highly collectible and much-loved magical stories inspire a love of reading to last a lifetime.

www.rainbowmagicbooks.co.uk

"Rainbow Magic got my daughter reading chapter books. Great sparkly covers, cute fairies and traditional stories full of magic that she found impossible to put down" – Mother of Edie (6 years)

"Florence LOVES the Rainbow Magic books. She really enjoys reading now" Mother of Florence (6 years)

The Rainbow Magic
Reading Challenge

Well done, fairy friend – you have completed the book!
This book was worth 10 points.

See how far you have climbed on the **Reading Rainbow**
on the Rainbow Magic website below.

The more books you read, the more points you will get,
and the closer you will be to becoming a Fairy Princess!

How to get your Reading Rainbow
1. Cut out the coin below
2. Go to the Rainbow Magic website
3. Download and print out your poster
4. Add your coin and climb up the Reading Rainbow!

There's all this and lots more at
www.rainbowmagicbooks.co.uk

You'll find activities, competitions, stories, a special
newsletter and complete profiles of all the
Rainbow Magic fairies. Find a fairy with your name!